1001

by Jason Grote

A SAMUEL FRENCH ACTING EDITION

SAMUEL FRENCH

FOUNDED 1830

NEW YORK HOLLYWOOD LONDON TORONTO

SAMUELFRENCH.COM

IMPORTANT BILLING AND CREDIT
REQUIREMENTS

1001 was workshopped and had its word premiere in 2007 at the Denver Center Theatre Company Kent Thompson, Artistic Director.

Original New York City Production produced by Page 73 Productions in association with Doug Nevin, Caroline Prugh and Erica Lynn Schwartz

1001 was first produced in January 2007 at The Denver Center Theater, Denver Colorado, with the following cast:

A . . . . Lanna Joffrey
B . . . . Daoud Heidami
C . . . . Josh Philip Weinstein
D . . . . Jeanine Serralles
E . . . . Drew Cortese
F . . . . John Livingstone Rolle

Directed by Ethan McSweeny
Scenic design by Rachel Hauck
Costume design by Murrell Horton
Lighting Design by Charles R. MacLeod
Sound Design by Matthew C. Swartz
Dramaturgy by Allison Horsley
Movement Coach, Robert Davidson
Fight Director, Geoffrey Kent
Assistant Director, Anthony Luciano
Dialect Coaches, Kathryn G. Maes and Douglas W. Montequin
DJ, Sara Thurston

1001 received its New York premiere in October 2007 at the Rose Nagelberg Theater, New York, NY, produced by P73 Productions, with the following cast:

A . . . . Roxanna Hope
B . . . . Jonathan Hova
C . . . . Matthew Rauch
D . . . . Mia Barron
E . . . . Drew Cortese
F . . . . John Livingstone Rolle

Directed by Ethan McSweeny
Scenic projection design by Rachel Hauck
Costume design by Murell Horton
Lighting design by Tyler Micoleau
Sound design by Lindsay Jones
Assistant Director, Anthony Luciano
Original Music & DJ Spinning by DJ Arisa Sound

CHARACTERS

A - Female, 20s/early 30s, Middle Eastern. Plays **SCHEHERAZADE** and **DAHNA**

B - Male, 30s-40s, any ethnicity (diversity STRONGLY encouraged). Plays **THE ONE-EYED ARAB, JUML'S MASTER, MOSTAFA, A SLAVE, SINDBAD, VOICE OF ALAN DERSHOWITZ,** and the **DJINN.**

C - Male. 20s/early 30s, Caucasian, plays **SHAHRIYAR** and **ALAN**

D - Female, 20s/30s, any ethnicity (diversity STRONGLY encouraged). Plays **THE VIRGIN BRIDE, DUNYAZADE, THE PRINCESS MARIDAH, JUML, KUCHUK HANEM,** and **LUBNA**

E - Male, 30s-40s, any ethnicity (diversity STRONGLY encouraged). Plays **JORGE LUIS BORGES, THE EMIR GHASSAN, THE HORRIBLE MONSTER, OSAMA BIN LADEN,** and **WAZIR**

F - Male, 20s/30s, any ethnicity (diversity STRONGLY encouraged). Plays **YAHYA AL-HUSAYNI, ASSER, GUSTAVE FLAUBERT, THE ORTHODOX JEWISH STUDENT, VOICE OF MODERATOR,** and **A EUNUCH**

TIME AND PLACE

Various, represented minimally. This is intended as a trunk show, with six actors playing all of the roles. Doubling is deliberate and most costume and scene changes should take place in full view of the audience. Location is indicated by oral storytelling, simple costume pieces, hand props, etc. The two primary locations are the fantasized Medieval Persia of the Arabian Nights stories and New York City in the present and near future, but the play goes everywhere.

A COUPLE OF NOTES

Occasionally this play is misread. In this misreading, the modern-day, Alan and Dahna story is the "real" one, and that everything else is somehow "fake." This is a mistake, especially as regards the staging of the play. The stakes are always extremely high and the proceedings are always very serious, regardless of the presence of jokes, heightened language, or flights of fancy. By the same token, there are elements of fantasy in the modern-day scenes as well, and these should not be ignored – every scene in the play (as in life) is "real" and "fake" in roughly equal measure.

Also, there is a brief throwaway gag in scene 11, in which Osama bin Laden recites a little bit of a popular song. There is the temptation here to overdetermine the joke and have everyone do a sort of Michael Jackson dance. Please do not do this. Everyone in the cast will want to do it – what group of actors wouldn't like to have this sort of fun in rehearsal? But the joke isn't built to withstand the length and duration that this will involve, plus it doesn't really have anything to do with the play, and it will distract from the ideas of the piece in a way that is ultimately destructive.

SPECIAL THANKS TO

Liesl Tommy, Daniel Aukin, Alexandra Conley, and Sarah Benson at Soho Rep, for their support and work in the conception and initial development of the play.

Wendy Goldberg, David M. White, and the extraordinary staff and interns at the O'Neill Playwrights' Conference; Kent Thompson, Bruce Sevey, and Chad Henry at Denver Center Theater; Liz Jones, Asher Richelli, Nicole Fix, and Daniel Shiffman of P73 Productions; Gavin Witt and Otis Ramsey-Zoe at Baltimore Center Stage; Ed Herendeen at the Contemporary American Theater Festival; Sharon Ott; Kristin Gandrow; Lisa Timmel, and Mark Fleischer, for all of their help in further developing the play.

Ethan McSweeny for his excellent productions in Denver and New York.

Antje Oegel for being such a wise, passionate, and devoted advocate of the play.

Daoud Heidami for the Arabic phrases.

(A slash ("/") in the dialogue indicates an interruption, and the next line should begin there.)

(This is a trunk show; it should be able to be performed on a bare stage, with a trunk or two filled with costumes, props, draperies.)

(If there is a set, it should evoke mazes, impossible architecture, endless spirals descending ever upward or downward; think an M.C. Escher drawing, the view-from-above of the staircase in Hitchcock's Vertigo, *the dizzyingly elaborate ceilings of Persian mosques, or the labyrinthine back alleys of East Jerusalem or Cairo; whatever it is, it should induce mild inertia.)*

(About the scene titles: there are times when they should be shared with the audience, but not always. Perhaps they are said aloud by the entire cast in unison, like a chorus. Perhaps they are shown as projections or by cast members holding signs.)

(It would be nice to have music playing under as many scenes as possible.)

0. Prologue (Scheherazade in Times Square)

(Enter A *as* SCHEHERAZADE, *an Arab woman, in a business suit. She carries with her an enormous, dusty Islamic tome, and she acts out what the* ENSEMBLE *narrates: walking through Times Square in the present or near future. She speaks with no Arabic accent.)*

(The following may be split between different performers, though performer A *should be favored where appropriate.)*

ENSEMBLE. Scheherazade stands in the center of the world and thinks: This is it? The land of milk and honey?

She tip-toes through the throngs of fat crusaders. Tip. Tip. Tip.

Here all is ifrits and djinns, flitting to and fro, illuminating an infinity of idols.

She has been told of them, these djinns and ifrits, conjured by the infidels.

This is why she bears the story that weighs so heavily on her back and her hips. It moves inside her. Feel it? Feel it move. It is the story of a final jihad against the infidel (insh'Allah)

Or it is the story of a monstrous carriage crashing into one of these great stone fortresses

Or it is the story of a stone named Plu-to-ni-um that comes apart faster and faster in tiny bits, a stone that unleashes holy cleansing fire

Or it is

(She opens the book. The world ends [this can be cheesy].)

(Blackout.)

(A shines a flashlight under her face.)

A/SCHEHERAZADE. There is only one story. It has always ever been thus. The story is comprised of every word that has ever been or will ever be uttered. It is an elaborate maze, a trap from which there is no way to break free, for nothing exists outside of it. No story, no you.

Witness:

1. The One-Eyed Arab

(**B** *sits as* **THE ONE-EYED ARAB**, *as if in front of a tent in a bazaar. He may or may not be Middle Eastern, and clearly has both his eyes.*)

(*During this, ensemble members dress* **C** *as* **SHAHRIYAR**, *a fearsome warrior king.*)

B/ONE-EYED ARAB. Come! Come, sit! You like tea? Boy! Two teas. I see the lady is looking at my lace. For you, special price. Three dinar. I see you are looking at my missing eye. By Allah, do not be ashamed. There is a story behind the missing eye, but you are busy, we save this for another time. You like boys? Tea! Two boys. Come, sit. I shall share with you a story, bism'Allah, the story of the great Persian king and his famous wife Scheherazade. Come, sit.

(*Sounds of a porn film.* **C/SHAHRIYAR** *seethes, watching it.*)

B/ONE-EYED ARAB. There was a great king, Shahriyar, whose queen had been adulterous with a filthy blackamoor slave, hideous of visage, his lips like an open pot, a leper and a paralytic to boot, lying as he was atop a strew of sugarcane trash, wrapped in the foulest of rags and tatters, for debauched women prefer the Moors on account of the size of their parts.

(*Out on* **C/SHAHRIYAR**, *porn sounds are cut short.*)

B/ONE-EYED ARAB. Revealed to Shahriyar was (by Allah) the lascivious heart of a whore beating as it does beneath the sweet breast of all women (except our mothers and grandmothers, who have never lain with men, praise be to Allah), and developed he a plan; each day he would wed a virgin, deflower the sweet child, and the next morning behead her before she had the chance to succumb to the corruption of Shaytan that threatens us all, *Auzhoo Billah min el Shaytan el-rajeem.*
I see you are looking at my missing boy.
I see you are looking at my missing lace.
I see you are looking at my missing story.

2. The Tale of Shahriyar, Part One

(Up on **C/SHAHRIYAR**, *savage and covered now in blood. He stands with* **D**, *as a* **VIRGIN** *– a young girl of 13 or 14, who trembles, crying. She may or may not be dressed in lavish medieval Islamic bridal gear, though it should look heartbreakingly like she is a kid playing dress-up. She has a strand of brightly-colored flowers woven into her hair. They are in Shahriyar's bedchamber.)*

(Something isn't right with **C** *– it is as if he is forgetting Shahriyar's lines, or isn't even sure what the play is.)*

C/SHAHRIYAR. Why do you cry? Look around you. All you could uh wish for. Jewels. Soft drinks no what do you call them soft Fabrics. The fruits of a thousand nations and one nation. Your every need attended to by an army of um unicorns no Eunuchs. The shattering love of a of a king. Come.

(She goes to him.)

D/VIRGIN. *(hysterical)* I do not I do not want

C/SHAHRIYAR. Sh. Whatever it is you fear, thank Alan uh Allah for averting what might have been worse.

D/VIRGIN. I I I we speak of them Of my sisters they who have married you and have come in here and have not returned. We do not know what has become of them but in the alleys and the markets there are whispers, we do not speak loudly of these things for we do not want to anger The We do not want to anger The You. My. Husband.

C/SHAHRIYAR. Cease weeping, for all is the will of. Allah. It is a great thing to have our souls released when they are still young and know not the sin and travail of this. World.

(He plays with the strand of flowers in her hair.)

You have nothing to fear from me. You smell lovely. Of sandalwood and vanilla. Like that moisturizer she. But she said it was. Unscented.

*(**C** stops short. Even he's not sure what he's talking about.)*

D/VIRGIN. My my mother. She wove these into my hair, these flowers. My father is a merchant and poor, these are for him three months' recompense. She she was worried. That you were. Displeased. With my sisters and. She.

C/SHAHRIYAR. Sh. I was not displeased with your lovely sisters and I am not uh displeased with you. Do not fear me. I am genital gentile No. Gentle.

(beat; shocked with himself)

I really am gentle what am I…

(…doing here?)

D/VIRGIN. King?

C/SHAHRIYAR. Nothing I.

(shakes it off)

Come.

(He kisses her. They both begin to relax. As **THE ONE-EYED ARAB** *narrates, they make love.)*

B/ONE-EYED ARAB. And so it went. Each night, a new bride, each night a honeymoon! The King had eradicated the problem of adultery. But, the next morning:

(In the bedchamber, morning, bird sounds. The **VIRGIN** *is giddy.)*

D/VIRGIN. My husband. I was so afeared of you. I thought that you would. But. Those hands. Your mouth. I know you would not.

(C/SHAHRIYAR kisses her fingers. He is silent.)

C/SHAHRIYAR. Close your. Eyes.

D/VIRGIN. Why.

C/SHAHRIYAR. Obey your husband. My um queen.

D/VIRGIN. All right.

(C/SHAHRIYAR whispers a short prayer.)

D/VIRGIN. My lord?

I have been thinking about the silk that is hanging in the tea room. It is red, and I worry that such a heated color will make our guests anxious. What would you think of blue silk? I imagine a deep blue, almost indigo, like the desert sky at dusk.

(He takes a scimitar from a hiding place. The scimitar is filthy. Red-brown with old blood and rust.)

C/SHAHRIYAR. Blue would be uh. Nice.

D/VIRGIN. Very good! I shall speak to the Vizier after breakfast.

C/SHAHRIYAR. Don't trouble yourself. I'll speak with him.

D/VIRGIN. Shahriyar? I am sorry for last night. What a silly girl I was! My mother warned me not to be so bird-witted. She was concerned that I would anger you with my foolishness. Now I feel as I am a woman!

C/SHAHRIYAR. That is because you uh you um. Are.

(He brings the sword down on her. Blackout.)

B/ONE-EYED ARAB. I fear, my guests, that my story has troubled you. Do not weep for this girl, friends, for only Allah is merciful, this life is suffering, to be released from it a kindness. Still, the Persians feared for the loss of their sisters and daughters, for Shahriyar's appetites were great and his anger protracted. Witness:

3. The Tale of Shahriyar, Part Two

*(C as **SHAHRIYAR** and E as his vizier, **WAZIR,** in the throne room. **E/WAZIR** holds deep blue silk and a small, neatly wrapped box.)*

E/WAZIR. My lord. The silk for the tea room has arrived. As well as.

*(**C/SHAHRIYAR** grabs the silk from him and lays it out on his lap. He takes the box, lays it on the cloth, and opens it. He reaches inside and gently pulls out a lock of hair– it is clearly the Virgin's hair, with the flowers woven into it. He smells it, puts his face in the box and kisses her head.)*

C/SHAHRIYAR. Do you like the cloth. My dear.

(beat)

Wazir. What does this cloth remind you of.

E/WAZIR. China. Perhaps. Or the road on the mountains through the Hindoo/ Kush –

C/SHAHRIYAR. The color.

E/WAZIR. My lord?

(beat)

It reminds me of death. My king. It reminds me of a blind and petulant child. Who is attempting to comfort himself with. Empty gestures and. Cheap consolation. Instead of peering into the void that has taken the place of his soul.

(pause)

C/SHAHRIYAR. It doesn't remind you of the desert sky at dusk?

E/WAZIR. …

C/SHAHRIYAR. Send it back and quarter the jackal who dared bring it to me. My orders were very specific, were they not? Blue like the desert sky at dusk. Not. Not cerulean, or…what is this? Cobalt? Periwinkle?

C/SHAHRIYAR. *(cont.)* It doesn't remind me of the desert sky at dusk either. But it reminds me of.

Something is not right. None of this is supposed to.

What the fuck!

(He tosses the cloth aside, pouting. E/WAZIR looks bewildered at the outburst and strange words.)

E/WAZIR. May I speak freely, my lord.

C/SHAHRIYAR. …

E/WAZIR. The sultanate. People are beginning to become. Upset. About your connubial proclivities. There are rustlings among the clerics, and. May we not take your future wives from the women of the Greeks or. The Mongols, even. The South Seas possess beautiful.

C/SHAHRIYAR. Only good Muslims, Wazir, right? Otherwise what is the um. Point.

E/WAZIR. Among the Persians and Arabs there are few left to marry to you or anyone. Save children, saplings who will not even bleed their first for many months yet. Or withered crones whose organs are as dry as the great desert to the south.

C/SHAHRIYAR. And your daughters. Right, Wazir?

E/WAZIR. …

C/SHAHRIYAR. Relax. I have no designs on your daughters Scheherazade or Dunyazade. That is what this is about, isn't it?

(*pause*)

The women of our sultanate, our wives, they don't sin anymore, do they? Before the days of Shahriyar the sultanate was a ceviche, no, a a cesspool of of uh iniquity, all men blind to the hustling of their wives, to and fro, eager to be penetrated by knaves, heathens, and what do you call it, blackamoors. But now?

E/WAZIR. They are perhaps dead. Or they sin still. We do not/know.

C/SHAHRIYAR. Freed from from sin. I don't expect to be liked, Wazir.

(*hands him the box*)

Put it with the others.

And I'll keep the silk. It reminds me of. Something.

(*BLACKOUT*)

B/ONE-EYED ARAB. And so our Wazir, worried father of Scheherazade and Dunyazade, did his duty. He moved the girl into her new home: a dank room, filled with boxes, wherein lived her thousand sisters and one.

4. Scheherazade Lights the Lights, Part Two

(*Up on* **E/WAZIR**, *in a dank room.*)

(**A** *enters, as* **SCHEHERAZADE**.)

A/SCHEHERAZADE. This is his harem?

The smell in here is vile.

E/WAZIR. You should not be in here at all.

A/SCHEHERAZADE. Why? Are you concerned that I might find out that his majesty is a butcher, that this palace is an abattoir, that I might tell of this to the sultanate, who have lost already a thousand daughters and one?

E/**WAZIR.** Stay your tongue.

A/**SCHEHERAZADE.** You are blind, father. Can you not see our sultanate crumbling at the edges, like paint peeling from a disused minaret? Men amass in the mosques. And talk. Clerics and soldiers, men long loyal to Shahriyar. You try to ply him with...what? Aphorisms? When meanwhile in a matter of weeks our great king shall awaken with hot irons in his eyes, his silken sheets soaked in blood or worse. And we, dear father? Your head will be shoved onto a spike and paraded in the market. Dunyazade and I will be lucky if we are raped to death.

E/**WAZIR.** Silence!

A/**SCHEHERAZADE.** You disappoint me, father. That you lack the courage to save our lives and his. I have taken matters into my own hands.

E/**WAZIR.** What have you done.

A/**SCHEHERAZADE.** Not an act of violence. Against any but myself, in any case.

E/**WAZIR.** You have not.

(**F** *enters, as a* **EUNUCH**.)

F/**EUNUCH.** My lord vizier. His majesty Shahriyar demands your presence.

E/**WAZIR.** *(hisses at* **SCHEHERAZADE**) This is not a game!

A/**SCHEHERAZADE.** It is not?

(beat)

Choose wisely, father. All rests now in your trust in me.

(E/**WAZIR** *and* F/**EUNUCH** *go to the King.*)

5. The Tale of Shahriyar, Part Three

(E/**WAZIR** *bows before* C/**SHAHRIYAR**.)

C/**SHAHRIYAR.** Uh Wazir.

E/**WAZIR.** Your majesty.

C/**SHAHRIYAR.** Your daughter has done a very unusual thing.

E/WAZIR. I am sorry, King.

C/SHAHRIYAR. She is beautiful, your daughter. But kind of. Weird, you know?

In any case, I honor my agreements. I don't want your child's blood on my hands. But she has come to me thusly:

6. Scheherazade Lights the Lights, Part One

(Up on **A/SCHEHERAZADE:** *)*

A/SCHEHERAZADE. Shahriyar!

(as if washing him with her spit, like a mom)

Look at you. Dried blood in the deep cracks around your eyes and mouth. And here, in the folds between your fingers.

(She licks between his fingers.)

I can feel the sinew in your arms. You have been lifting a heavy sword. And often are you bringing it down. Am I correct?

C/SHAHRIYAR. You are. Very familiar to me. With me. To me.

Your hair. The shape of your nose.

You totally remind me of my girlfriend.

(beat; he shakes it off)

Does your father know where you are?

A/SCHEHERAZADE. My father does not know many things these days, does he?

C/SHAHRIYAR. Smart girl. You are bold and blast furnace. Blasphemous. Your father needs to give you a beating.

A/SCHEHERAZADE. I would prefer, my lord, were you to administer it.

C/SHAHRIYAR. Child. You don't know what you're asking for.

A/SCHEHERAZADE. I am the same age as you.

C/SHAHRIYAR. You live in the palace. You know what happens here.

A/SCHEHERAZADE. *(feeling his arms)* One night as a queen. One night in those arms, like twin ships' masts, then to be torn in twain by them like a spring lamb. To be consumed by you and forever sainted. This is what I want.

I have thought about this for a long time.

(pause)

C/SHAHRIYAR. I will speak to your father.

A/SCHEHERAZADE. I will not accept no for your answer. I will die by your hand as your sacrificed bride or will douse myself and my quarters in sailors' rum and put a candle to my hijab, by Allah, and take you and all this to paradise with me. And you shall be my husband there if not here.

(beat)

(C/SHAHRIYAR *kisses her violently.)*

C/SHAHRIYAR. I will speak to your father.

7. The Tale of Shahriyar, Part Three, continued

C/SHAHRIYAR. I am sorry, Wazir.

E/WAZIR. She is a stubborn girl.

Perhaps she would learn from the hand of a strong husband.

C/SHAHRIYAR. I'm afraid that she wouldn't have time to learn much.

(pause)

E/WAZIR. Do as you will, my King.

C/SHAHRIYAR. You know what you're consenting to.

E/WAZIR. Does one ever. My lord.

B/ONE-EYED ARAB. *(as if he's eaten nothing but chickpeas for years)* And so the two were wed. There was a great feast, even greater than the king's usual daily marriages; affairs of state were suspended. Beyond the palace was great mourning for this, the last of Persia's marriageable women. Inside, Shahriyar snapped his fingers, and a great pot of water was brought to him by his eunuchs. He and his bride cleansed their hands therein and dried them on a boy's head. Served were Shami apples and Osmani quinces, cucumbers of Nile growth, vetches of a Damascene ram, Egyptian limes and Sultani oranges and citrus; Aleppine jasmine, scented myrtle berries, flower of privet and chamomile, blood-red anemones, womb of an unfarrowed calf, violets, pomegranate bloom, a bull's eye, a twelve-cubit lobster, eglantine and narcissus, a goose and two mullets. Scheherazade was anointed in sandalwood oil, clad in bridal dress and veil of deep blue cloth, sapphires drawn across her forehead. Her eyes wild like the gazelle's as she executed her plan to save herself and the sultanate.

8. One Thousand Nights and One Night, Part One

(Shahriyar's bedchamber. **A/SCHEHERAZADE,** *cleans Shahriyar's sword as* **D** *(as her sister* **DUNYAZADE***), watches.* **DUNYAZADE** *wears a burqa that covers her entire body, face included.* **A/SCHEHERAZADE** *may have taken off some or most of her bridal clothing. Near them is the dusty Islamic tome.)*

*(**C/SHAHRIYAR** enters. Watches.)*

C/SHAHRIYAR. What are you doing?

A/SCHEHERAZADE. Have you cleaned this blade even once since you have begun to use it? It is a disgrace. I will not have the blood and bile of a thousand and one brides befoul the blade that penetrates me.

C/SHAHRIYAR. *(weirded out)* ...Okay.

(beat)

Call me king. You are disrespectful, I am the King, you're supposed to call me king or your majesty or. Something.

A/SCHEHERAZADE. King. Do you not tire of the daughters of nobles, sold to you like livestock, cowering in a corner as you bare your kingly fangs?

C/SHAHRIYAR. A king doesn't marry because he wants a challenge.

A/SCHEHERAZADE. It seems as if you know little about what kings are supposed to do.

(She hands him the polished sword, begins to disrobe and seduce him. He notices D/DUNYAZADE.)

C/SHAHRIYAR. Who is that?

A/SCHEHERAZADE. My sister, Dunyazade.

D/DUNYAZADE. I do not wish to disturb you or be immodest in your presence, my lord, Allah be praised.

C/SHAHRIYAR. What is she doing here What are you doing here?

A/SCHEHERAZADE. Sister?

D/DUNYAZADE. *(all in one breath)* Begging your pardon my king my sister tells me stories each night before we sleep I beg mercy of your greatness for I know that after tonight I shall no longer hear the glorious stories of my sister Scheherazade and I beg you to allow her to tell me one last story for I shall never more hear her tell of them was that correct sister?

A/SCHEHERAZADE. Yes, Dunyazade. A final mercy. Your "majesty." Before you lie with me.

C/SHAHRIYAR. Okay. And tell her she can take that

(loudly, as if D is deaf or foreign)

You can take that thing off!

A/SCHEHERAZADE. And now, a story.

Stand in front of me now king, and look closely at my face. My full red lips, my wet mouth, my nose, and each eye.

Gaze like the Sufis do when they spin and eat their hashish and stare into the endless black sky of the desert night. Do you see what they see?

C/SHAHRIYAR. Yes it's like a. Like a screen saver or.

(She picks up the tome and opens it. It as if the storm she describes is rising from the pages.)

A/SCHEHERAZADE. A distant colorful storm, from an infinity away: is it a mirage? Watch as it comes closer, eating the sky, consuming all in its jagged green flames. Sit, o king, as I reveal to you:

9. The Tale of Yahya Al-Husayni amongst the Dead

(**B** and **E** enter as **FEMALE SLAVES**, and begin to undress
and make over **D**, who is now **THE PRINCESS MARI-
DAH**. **F** enters as **PRINCE YAHYA**, watching obsessively.
B and **E** remove **D**'s burqa, and dress her in a jilbab (a
sort of Syrian pantsuit), deep blue, the same fabric as
Shahriyar's silk.)

A/SCHEHERAZADE. There once was a Syrian prince, by
Allah, who from his boyhood was madly in love with
his own twin sister.

F/YAHYA. (addressing audience) Her forehead was flower-
white; her eyes were like those of the wild heifer, with
eyebrows like the crescent moon which ends Sha'aban
and begins Ramazan; her mouth was the ring of Sulay-
man, her lips coral-red, and her teeth like a line of
chamomile petals. Her breasts, like two pomegranates
of even size, stood at bay, as her body rose and fell in
waves. Her navel would have held an ounce of benzoin
ointment.

(to **MARIDAH**, as a child)

Now come, sister, and bear witness as to what lies in
my trousers.

(**D** and **F** become **MARIDAH** and **YAHYA** as children, in a
hiding place. **MARIDAH** looks at his crotch.)

(**MARIDAH** has a lisp.)

D/MARIDAH. Brother?

(noticing)

Oh.

It ith a thtrange thing, and frightening.

F/YAHYA. When one touches it it grows large, like unto the
great minaret over yonder.

D/MARIDAH. (not interested) Interethting.

F/YAHYA. Touch it, sister. Be not affrighted.

Here.

(He puts her hand on him.)

D/MARIDAH. Oh! It growth.

(*She continues.*)

D/MARIDAH. When will it grow to the thize of yonder mina-ret?

F/YAHYA. Soon. Keep on.

(*She starts to get bored. He appears to be enjoying himself.*)

D/MARIDAH. It hath grown but thtill it ith not the thize of the minaret. It ith not hardly the thize of a thmall Lebanethe pickle of the thort therved with olive and chick-pea.

F/YAHYA. Sh. Come close to me.

Oh.

D/MARIDAH. (*what's up with him?*) Brother?

(**E** *enters as their father,* **THE EMIR GHASSAN**, *cutting off* **YAHYA**'s *orgasm.*)

E/GHASSAN. What manner of mischief is this?

F/YAHYA. Father. I. It was her idea she

(**GHASSAN** *cuffs him.*)

E/GHASSAN. You are but little ones, so this transgression I shall forgive, but it shall not happen again, insh'Allah. Know that this is a foul thing you have done.

(*all menace*)

Leave me alone with your sister.

(*out on them*)

A/SCHEHERAZADE. And yet the Prince could not contain his lust for his sister and sin befell between them, even unto adulthood.

(*Up on the ledge of a very high minaret.* **GHASSAN** *holds a terrified, vertigo-suffering* **YAHYA** *out of the window.*)

A/SCHEHERAZADE. Yahya al-Husayni was afeared of high places; and so, the Emir brought his son to the top of the minaret of the great Mosque, and held him from a ledge, whereby he could see all of everything , laid out before him against the deep blue canvas of the desert sky at dusk.

E/GHASSAN. If I let you go you will fall from such a great height that it is as a height found in our dreams, and a fall from here shall never end. But I will not let you go. I will fasten irons to your wrists and ankles and have you watch as your twin sister Maridah is thrown from here. And I shall leave you here for a thousand days and one day, until the djinn-madness that possesses you to hump your very sister like a vexed baboon shall be made real madness. Do you understand.

F/YAHYA. *(panic)* Uh

E/GHASSAN. *(cold)* I love you my son.

Do not disappoint me.

(GHASSAN brings him back inside. Out on them.)

A/SCHEHERAZADE. But the Emir's threats were to no avail, for Yahya was consumed with desire for the flesh of his flesh. He forged a plan: none would expect him to rendezvous with Maridah in the very minaret that would be the spot of his father's threatened torment. From here, all could be seen; the Emir's arrival would be heralded by a great procession led by horsemen, torch-bearers, and unusually agile midgets. He sent to his twin a cryptic and anonymous letter.

(Up on YAHYA, struggling against his vertigo to climb the infinite stairs of the minaret.)

A/SCHEHERAZADE. Yahya al-Husayni struggled with every step, fighting dizziness and nausea, even committing the blasphemy of praying to Allah to give him the very strength to sin against Him.

(YAHYA gets to the top of the minaret and puts the burqa over himself. He sits in the dark.)

A/SCHEHERAZADE. He sat in the dark, awaiting the arrival of his Other.

(MARIDAH enters the dim minaret, alone and scared.)

(beat)

D/MARIDAH. Who ith it? Who ith there?

F/YAHYA. Maridah. It is I.

(He removes the burqa.)

D/MARIDAH. Yahya!

F/YAHYA. We need no more be apart.

D/MARIDAH. We muthtn't. Father will thend me to death. And you to madneth.

F/YAHYA. He will not look for us here. All the world knows of my fear of great height.

D/MARIDAH. That ith right. How fare you now?

F/YAHYA. It is difficult. But to see you, I am filled with joy. Maridah, come to me.

D/MARIDAH. Thith ith a Mothque. A holy plathe. What we do ith the greatetht of thinth.

F/YAHYA. It is all the sweeter for that, is it not?

(He pulls her close.)

D/MARIDAH. Oh, Yahya. Quite thoft you are. I had forgotten.

F/YAHYA. Let me breathe the sandalwood odor of your hair.

(D and F may or may not do the following:)

A/SCHEHERAZADE. She kissed him on his closed eyelids. He opened her jilbab and kissed her on her throat. They loved one another sweetly, sensually, for sheer mutual delight in their own expensive smell. Then she pushed him away.

(D does this.)

F/YAHYA. Do not stop.

D/MARIDAH. Thith ith not how I wanted thith to happen. You believe I love you. And when you lothe me, you will know that I wanted to go on loving you.

F/YAHYA. I will not lothe you. Lose you.

E/GHASSAN. *(in darkness)* You will.

F/YAHYA. Father?

(GHASSAN enters, from behind MARIDAH.)

F/YAHYA. How did this happen? We should have seen you coming.

E/GHASSAN. The eye of your father is everywhere.

(He chains **YAHYA** *to the ledge.)*

F/YAHYA. Father. No. FATHER!

(He tosses the screaming **MARIDAH** *out the window as* **YAHYA** *watches.)*

A/SCHEHERAZADE. And so Ghassan al-Husayni threw his daughter Maridah to her death. She did not fall in perpetuum as promised, but fell against one outcropping and another and another until she lay limp and bent atop the roof of a gardener's hut.

Yahya's father left him cinched to the ledge for one thousand days and one day.

(A **GUARD** *roughly slaps a long, fake beard, and perhaps some make-up and tooth black, onto* **YAHYA.**)

A/SCHEHERAZADE. Finally, the thousandth day and one arrived, and the Emir had his son taken down. All attempted to speak with Yahya of his recent suffering, but the Prince sat, silent.

*(***GUARD** *removes beard and perhaps dresses* **YAHYA** *sin the blue silk. He sits, catatonic.)*

A/SCHEHERAZADE. He began to wander down to the market, and word got out that the mad son of the Emir walked therein. All came to gawk at the helpless ninnyhammer who might once have ruled them. That was when he saw her.

*(***D** *enters as* **JUML,** *a slave girl, holding a jug of water on her head.* **YAHYA** *spots her.)*

F/YAHYA. Maridah?

A/SCHEHERAZADE. He followed her, though she was not his sister Maridah, but Juml, a slave-girl.

*(***JUML** *walks [perhaps in place?], with* **YAHYA** *at her back, gaping at her.)*

A/SCHEHERAZADE. Juml sensed the mad prince at her back and turned down this narrow alley and that throughout the great labyrinthine city in her attempt to avoid his bedeviled gaze. But he followed her all the way back to the house of her master.

D/JUML. *(into house)* It is I! Juml! Let me in!
I am here! Juml! With the water!

F/YAHYA. Do not shout.

D/JUML. *(to* **YAHYA***)* You must go. They are coming soon for I have been sent to fetch the well water and I am late, and they are likely to be thirsty and unclean.

(He touches her curiously, like he is inspecting a horse.)

F/YAHYA. Know you who I am?

D/JUML. No.

(beat)

Yes. They speak of you. In the alleys and stalls of the marketplace.

F/YAHYA. And what is it they say?

D/JUML. I cannot say, Sire.
It can not be true in any case, for they say you do not speak.

F/YAHYA. I have not spoken for a very long time. So what they say must be true. It must be true that I am a mad prince, demented. Chewed and swallowed by my father and shat out as a chucklehead. Yes?

*(***B*** enters, as Juml's* **MASTER** *and grabs her by the hair.)*

B/MASTER. JUML! Get in here! Lazy girl. You are late! Don't bother the idiot prince.

(He reaches in his pocket and offers **YAHYA** *something.)*

B/MASTER. Here, majesty, a taffy.

F/YAHYA. Unhand her, sir.

B/MASTER. *(he talks?)* …Your majesty?

(confidentially)

With all respect, sire? The law states that all men shall treat their slaves as they will.

F/YAHYA. She is not yours anymore.

B/MASTER. Please, sire, I do not want to bring this matter to your father.

F/YAHYA. I will give you for her one thousand gold dinars.

B/**MASTER.** Sire. I can not accept/ this gift from –

F/**YAHYA.** You shall take for her one thousand gold dinars or I will use my newly-found gifts of speech and lucidity to have you flayed and your skin made into a saddle.

B/**MASTER.** *(petrified)* A thousand apologies, sire.

Her name is Juml. She is/ a skilled –

F/**YAHYA.** Her name is Maridah now.

A/**SCHEHERAZADE.** And so Prince Yahya brought the slave girl Juml back with him to the palace, where attendants washed, groomed, and dressed the girl as Yahya gazed. He began to transform her from who she was into who he wanted her to be.

(**B** *becomes a* **FEMALE SLAVE**, *washing and dressing* **JUML** *in blue silk.*)

F/**YAHYA.** That is not what I asked for.

Blue, like the desert sky at dusk. And the jilbab slightly shorter, so just a bit of the pants show. And tasseled side-slits, ending just below the knee.

B/**SLAVE.** Well. His majesty certainly knows what he wants!

E/**GHASSAN.** *(off)* Yahya?

F/**YAHYA.** *(to* SLAVE*)* Hide her! Now!

(*The* **SLAVE** *hides her.* **GHASSAN** *enters.*)

E/**GHASSAN.** Where is the girl?

(silence)

Be not fatuous, I know that you speak again.

F/**YAHYA.** *(panic)* How…?

(catching himself)

She is being groomed. She was a slave-girl with filth on her face, dirt underneath her fingernails, an odor like a she-mule.

E/**GHASSAN.** I will meet her this night, then, at the feast I will announce, to celebrate the convalescence of your reason.

F/**YAHYA.** *(thinking fast)* Feast? I. No feast, father, please. Now that my reason has returned I am sure to have hundreds of wives. It would be unseemly for a future Emir to celebrate his pairing with a single slave girl.

(Beat. **GHASSAN** *is suspicious.)*

E/GHASSAN. Very well.

It appears your reason has returned far beyond that which you had before.

*(**GHASSAN** stares him down, exits.)*

A/SCHEHERAZADE. Yahya kept his resurrected Other hidden from his father – and all, but a small retinue of loyal servants. He committed that act of ordinary magic that, every day, the powerful enact upon the powerless: he rewrote her story. Witness:

*(**JUML** emerges, bathed in green light, the spitting image **MARIDAH***. He takes her in.)*

(beat)

D/JUML. Thire. I mutht thpeak with you.

(This is hard for her.)

I can not do this. My Prince Yahya, they have told me who was this Maridah in whose image you have made me.

This is a dream, to go from a mere slave girl to the wife of a prince. But also this is a nightmare, to be made into your twin sister who also was your lover.

F/YAHYA. I shall hear nothing you say until you speak as Maridah.

(pause)

D/JUML. Pleathe, Yahya. I can not be who it ith you want me to be.

F/YAHYA. That is better.

Our love is no sin. Come to me.

(They kiss passionately.)

A/SCHEHERAZADE. But even this was not enough. He had to bring his new Maridah to the place where she had earlier left him; he had to bring her to the minaret.

(YAHYA and JUML enter the top of the minaret. YAHYA is woozy from the height, and from reliving his recent trauma.)

D/JUML. Thith ith it, ith it not? The tower at which your father held you prithoner.

(He breathes deeply, trying not to freak out.)

D/JUML. I would watch you up here. I mean Juml would, the thlave girl.

F/YAHYA. *(barely keeping it together)* Maridah. Our love has conquered death itself, and our father the Emir.
Have you the poem?
Read it, and I shall love you.

(As she recites the poem, he opens her garments and kisses her body.)

D/JUML. We are the raincloudth thtreaming pearlth

(He starts to go down on her.)

D/JUML. No. No Yahya no.

F/YAHYA. Keep reciting.

D/JUML. We are Oh we are the Treathury Of Thecretth
If you have become like night and Oh My night and thtorm
UNH
Oh My Oh My Yeth

(GHASSAN enters, cutting off the moment of orgasm.)

E/GHASSAN. What manner of mischief is this!

F/YAHYA. Father!?

(Lights out on them. SCHEHERAZADE stretches and yawns. C/SHAHRIYAR, stares at her.)

C/SHAHRIYAR. What happens? What does the father do?

A/SCHEHERAZADE. I am exhausted, my King. And we have business to attend to this night, do we not?

(She makes the "throat-slashing" gesture.)

C/SHAHRIYAR. You have to tell me what Uh happens. It sounds like a movie I uh.

A/SCHEHERAZADE. If you must hear it. But I do fear the ending would surpass your understanding.

C/SHAHRIYAR. What is that supposed to uh. Mean?

A/SCHEHERAZADE. I mean to cast no aspersion, majesty. I meant only that what the Emir Ghassan did then may only be understood if one first hears another story.

C/SHAHRIYAR. I don't uh What do you call it Care. Tell it.

A/SCHEHERAZADE. *(she's got him where she wants him)* Very well then. I bring you:

10. The Tale of Alan in His Labyrinth

*(As **A/SCHEHERAZADE** narrates, ensemble members dress **C** as **ALAN**, a modern-day hipster type who has been in a subway tunnel for some time. He has a head injury; perhaps he wears his dress shirt, the same color blue as the cloth in the earlier scenes, around his head. Dried blood should be visible through it. He wears work clothes of the type an arty temp or web programmer etc would wear. He is filthy.)*

A/SCHEHERAZADE. There once was or someday will be, insh'Allah, one Man Hat.

Like the ancient city of Babel, Man Hat grew spires that threatened to puncture the sky, endless structures of stone and glass.

Its true self was kept hidden in a labyrinthine underworld. A place of tunnels filled with filth and castoffs. There came a day when the sky shoved back at the great lifeless towers and the dead city collapsed under its own weight.

Man Hat was forced into the labyrinth

Forced to embrace its true self

If it had any hope of survival.

*(Dark. Sounds of dripping water. **ALAN** walks toward us but doesn't seem to get any closer.)*

C/ALAN. I don't know how long I was, or how I even Uh. But. Some things I. Like I remember I lived in a E train, between stations. It was so Uh dark. Pitch black, all the. I had no sense of. Time. But.

(beat)

Maybe I rushed down with a crowd when I heard the Or saw it actually, I would have seen or felt the light and burning wind, before the sound, you know, and maybe I ran under Citicorp Center maybe, before, um. Maybe I heard the sound of the building hitting the street, wiping out the shops along Lexington Avenue straight down past Grand Central or. Uh. I think I must have wanted to get away from the toxic. The cloud of vaporized PCs, burning uh carpet a black, hanging fog of particulate, blotting out the uh.

(beat)

Because I had water, matches, granola bars, and. Air freshener, for some. Reason. I don't know if I looted it or bought it But I guess I must have. Uh.

(beat)

It ran out quickly, the water, so I made a crude and uh, ineffective distillation thing out of. But you know, it didn't really, uh work. The water was dirty, gray. But still I.

(beat)

I was hungry, there were some chicken bones, I mean, the things you. I was used to like organic produce. I used to get so annoyed when those guys would eat wings and toss the bones under the, you know, but I was really Uh glad. Anyway I was sucking the dried bits of meat off and then it hit me: where were the rats? No skittering, no, uh, running across my, um, when I slept, you know. For the first time I noticed how quiet everything. I was hit with this, like a wall, the tremendous, monolithic, unavoidable fact of my complete and utter aloneness.

(beat)

I used to have a. Girlfriend. I would Uh feel the smooth skin on her shoulders and the nape of her neck. I still remember her smell, it was sandalwood, she swore she never wore anything but it was. In her hair. Which I remember. In my face when we slept and I would.

(beat; awed and sad)

Everyone.

(beat)

I walked. I felt blind after a while, like a bat or a mole.

(beat)

Then there were no tracks anymore. I didn't notice where they stopped just one day they were gone. The tunnel went on but it was like a cave, the walls were cold stone with water dripping from them. Sweet water. I would hold out my tongue and the water would drip onto it and it tasted good, fresh, not like the.

(beat)

I was starving but it felt far away, like someone else's hunger. And then. I saw. A light. It was like it was letting out, finally, into a trainyard, or. But it wasn't. A trainyard.

(ALAN *gradually emerges from the labyrinth into a bright, outdoor space. He is blinded. Sounds of an open-air Arabic marketplace.)*

I smelled it before my eyes adjusted. It could have been Atlantic Avenue; incense, cardamom, strawberry tobacco. Then, underneath: a thick wave of body odor; earthy smells of animal shit; an acidic stench of old uh. Roadkill.

(beat)

This isn't New York. That much is instantly. A man grabs me.

(B, *as* **THE ONE-EYED ARAB,** *grabs him.)*

B/ONE-EYED ARAB. *It fadal shuf esh fee endna it fadal!*
Come! Come, sit! You like tea? Boy! Two teas. I see you are looking at my missing eye. By Allah, do not be ashamed.

C/ALAN. He says, even though he's got both eyes. What is this place, I say.

B/ONE-EYED ARAB. It is the black market, Monsieur Alan,

C/ALAN. He says, I don't know how he knows my name,

B/ONE-EYED ARAB. A cluttered Arab street of bazaars, shops and stalls. On the surface, the atmosphere is merely languid, but there is the sinister undercurrent of illicit trade.

C/ALAN. Okay, I say. I ask him if he knows where I can get something to eat.

B/ONE-EYED ARAB. I know what you have come to see: the object of wonder, the box of ifrit, the container of light, great and sinful thing which I keep hidden in my stall. You have traveled with great difficulty, experiencing much sorrow and misfortune, and so I will show you.

C/ALAN. He hands me this enormous, dusty Islamic tome and he brings into this tent. And in the tent is a box with another blue cloth on it, and he takes the cloth off and under it there's a TV.

(**B** *does this. The screen is not visible to us, but* **ALAN** *is bathed in bluish TV light.* **B** *hands* **C** *an enormous, dusty Islamic tome.*)

C/ALAN. He nods solemnly and turns on the TV and on it it's hard to make out but I think it's

11. Monster Chiller Horror Theatre with Osama Bin Laden

(*On another part of the stage, we see what is on the TV;* **E** *dressed as* **OSAMA**, *as he usually appears in his videos. He sounds like Vincent Price.*)

(*A note about this scene: you should NOT telegraph the joke by playing "Thriller" underneath Osama's speech. It's fine to bring it in towards the end, but the audience should have time to let it sink in.*)

E/OSAMA. *(laughs villainously)*
For is it not as the great poets say:
Darkness Falls Across The Land
The Midnight Hour Is Close At Hand
Creatures Crawl In Search Of Blood

To Terrorize Yall's Neighborhood
And Whosoever Shall Be Found
Without The Soul For Getting Down
Must Stand And Face The Hounds Of Hell
And Rot Inside A Corpse's Shell
And Though You Fight To Stay Alive
Your Body Starts To Shiver
For No Mere Mortal Can Resist
The Evil Of

12. The Tale of Alan and Dahna, Part Four

*(We are suddenly in an apartment on the Upper West Side of Manhattan. A/**DAHNA**, a Palestinian-American graduate student, sits on a windowsill, smoking a cigarette out the window. **C**, still **ALAN**, uses the huge Islamic tome as if it is a laptop computer. A clicks a remote, turning off the "TV;" lights down on **E/OSAMA**. C seems to know where he is now.)*

(In the apartment are: the blue silk, a rubber snake, books.)

C/**ALAN.** I was watching that.

A/**DAHNA.** You're checking your e-mail.

C/**ALAN.** I was half-watching it.

A/**DAHNA.** What if I was gone?

C/**ALAN.** *(not paying attention)* Gone where.

A/**DAHNA.** What if that was all that was left of me? E-mail. Like if I went back to Gaza. Without you this time.

C/**ALAN.** Yeah.

I mean, I'm sorry, what?

A/**DAHNA.** Alan. There's something I have to tell you.

*(**C** closes the book/laptop.)*

C/**ALAN.** I'm sorry, that was rude of me. What were you saying?

A/**DAHNA.** I talked to my parents the other day.

(The intercom buzzes.)

C/ALAN. *(into intercom)* Hello?

D/DUNYAZADE. *(off)* UPS.

> *(He buzzes **D** in.)*

C/ALAN. You were saying.

A/DAHNA. My parents.

> They said they understood. What I was going through, my lifestyle, you know. They're not as. Intransigent. As you might think.

C/ALAN. I never thought they were/ intransigent, Dahna.

> *(There's a knock at the door.)*

C/ALAN. I got it.

> *(He opens the door. **D/DUNYAZADE** stands there, dressed in her burqa.)*

C/ALAN. Uh.

> Dahna?

> *(Without speaking, **D** slowly walks to **DAHNA** and hands her a corrugated cardboard box. It might look like the box with the head in it, from earlier. She turns to **ALAN** and shoves a UPS clipboard at him.)*

C/ALAN. Uh

> *(He signs for it.)*

> *(In a hail of styrofoam peanuts, **DAHNA** pulls a dusty, bejeweled golden lamp from the box.)*

C/ALAN. What is it?

A/DAHNA. I'm.

> I remember it from when I was a kid.

> It belonged to my uncle. But the thing is I never thought it was real, like a real memory. I always thought I dreamt it.

> *(**DUNYAZADE** goes to the laptop/tome and ceremoniously turns it back into a book. She opens it to a certain page; **A** looks over her shoulder.)*

C/ALAN. What's it say?

A/DAHNA. It says

13. One Thousand Nights and One Night, Part Three

*(As they enact the scene, the other performers dress **A** and*
*C as **SCHEHERAZADE** and **SHAHRIYAR**, respectively.)*

A/SCHEHERAZADE. Oh, my dear Shahriyar, surely you have heard your fill of stories. For many days have we lain here, hearing tales of faraway lands. Surely we may now sleep, and tomorrow I shall be released from this sinful world.

C/SHAHRIYAR. *(still **ALAN**, a little)* Um. I. No.

A/SCHEHERAZADE. No?

C/SHAHRIYAR. The story. I need to hear how it ends.

A/SCHEHERAZADE. Oh, which story, majesty? There are so many. The Tale of the Orientalists, the Tale of Brian and the Three Eunuchs, the Tale of Sinbad and the Show Time at the Palace of Apollo. Are there not things you must attend to?

C/SHAHRIYAR. No. I need to hear how it ends.

A/SCHEHERAZADE. But in order to make sense of the stories lain before you, you must first understand yet another tale.

C/SHAHRIYAR. I don't care.

A/SCHEHERAZADE. Very well, majesty. I bring you:

14. The Tale of Flaubert and His Mistress

*(**D** removes her burqa – underneath, she is **KUCHUK***
***HANEM**, the famous prostitute visited by Gustave Flau-*
bert during his travels in Egypt. She belly-dances, holding
*a snake that is obviously made of rubber. Note that **D** does*
not have to be a good, or even competent, belly-dancer,
and the snake dance should definitely look fake.)

A/SCHEHERAZADE. There once was, or will be, insh'Allah, a great infidel scribe. He was called Gustave Flaubert, a savage name, and he traveled over land and sea to arrive in the home of the famed courtesan Kuchuk Hanem.

*(F enters, as **FLAUBERT**, the 19th-century French author
of Madame Bovary. He writes furiously, occasionally
looking up to leer at **D**.)*

D/KUCHUK HANEM. He speaks little of my language. I speak
none of his. This is not unusual. I am a prostitute. I
have had many patrons, men of Cairo, merchants,
clerics. Bedouins, foreigners like this one.

You learn that words are not important. You learn to
notice a look, posture, the shape of an open mouth.
Sometimes they shudder when they touch you, Monsieur Gustave does this.

He is writing a letter.

F/FLAUBERT. Dear Mother:

Let me begin by giving you a great hug, so that I might
exhale the dusty, exotic air of Egypt into your lungs,
and you the cold wet air of Rouen into mine.

As I write this, darling, I sit on a divan in the House of
the famous courtesan Kuchuk Hanem. She is a splen-
did creature, with slightly coffee-colored skin, odor
of perspiration covered by sandalwood oil. When she
bends, her flesh ripples into bronze ridges. Her eyes
are dark and enormous. Her eyebrows black, her nos-
trils open and wide; heavy shoulders, full, apple-shaped
breasts. Her dance is brutal, savage.

*(**D** undoes **F**'s pants, and straddles him. They make love
under the blue silk.)*

F/FLAUBERT. Tonight I have my *coup* with Kuchuk, the first
of many. The flesh is as hard as bronze, and Kuchuk
has a resplendent arse. These shaved cunts make
a strange effect! Hers feels like rolls of velvet as she
makes me come.

Oh, mother, I feel like a tiger!

We stain the divan. She rolls over and falls asleep with
her hand in mine. She snores.

*(**D** does this.)*

F/FLAUBERT. At a late hour, perhaps three in the morning,
into our chamber a horrible monster drags himself!

(E *enters as* **THE HORRIBLE MONSTER**, *a withered old man, perhaps claiming to be Kuchuk's pimp. He does what* F *narrates.*)

F/FLAUBERT. He looks too enfeebled to be harmful, but I am unquiet as he ambles towards me. Kuchuk remains sleeping: is she used to this toad-eater? Is he her "fancy man?" He seizes my hand, which I snatch away before he can touch it with his lips, covered as they are in sores and a whitish slobber.

E/HORRIBLE MONSTER. Master…

F/FLAUBERT. He barely manages to wheeze,

E/HORRIBLE MONSTER. This is not a place for you.

F/FLAUBERT. I attempt to give him baksheesh out of a combination of pity and a desire to see him go, but he waves it away.

E/HORRIBLE MONSTER. It is not real. Listen. You must understand. I will tell you.

F/FLAUBERT. This poor pitiable creature seems to be telling me of the City of New York, of a University there. How he knows these things is impossible to understand. Oh, mother, where have I found myself?

E/HORRIBLE MONSTER. You try to make the Kuchuk Hanem into an experience to be purchased. You think the world is a restaurant. That every word is a word in a menu. Listen to my tale for it will tell you what you really are. I relate to you

15. The Tale of Dahna and Alan Dershowitz

(*A large lecture hall at Columbia University.* **A/DAHNA**, *is at a microphone during a Q&A session with the lawyer and professor* **ALAN DERSHOWITZ**.)

(*The following is FAST, lots of cross-talk. Actors may ad-lib where required.*)

E/HORRIBLE MONSTER. Across the many oceans, there was or will be, insh'Allah, a great place of learning where all came to ask questions of the wise man, a learned and powerful Jew, advisor to the Christian kings of America.

F/VOICE OF MODERATOR. *(offstage)* …Thank you, Professor Dershowitz. We'll have the next question, please.

E/HORRIBLE MONSTER. There came before the wise man a girl, Dahna, a student, schooled in the ways of infidels, but brave:

A/DAHNA. Yes, hello.

B/VOICE OF ALAN DERSHOWITZ. Hello.

A/DAHNA. Hi. I had a question about.

B/VOICE OF ALAN DERSHOWITZ. Yes.

A/DAHNA. I had a question about some of the claims you've been making about the campus divestiture/ movement –

B/VOICE OF ALAN DERSHOWITZ. The divestiture movement, yes, this is a campaign to get Universities to divest from Israeli companies, started by a very dangerously/ misguided group of –

A/DAHNA. I didn't yet ask my/ question –

B/VOICE OF ALAN DERSHOWITZ. I want to tell you– I want to tell you– are you a member of, are you involved with the campus divestiture group here at Columbia?

A/DAHNA. Yes, I am, but that isn't/ what I wanted to ask about –

B/VOICE OF ALAN DERSHOWITZ. This is a very, extremely hateful and extremist group of/ people here –

A/DAHNA. I am not– I am not extremist. If you'll/ just let me speak –

B/VOICE OF ALAN DERSHOWITZ. No, no, because the campaign for divestiture isn't intended to succeed.

A/DAHNA. It was a campaign for justice, based on/ the successful campaign against Apartheid in South Africa –

(Sounds of boos and perhaps some catcalls from the crowd.)

B/VOICE OF ALAN DERSHOWITZ. *(talking over her)* All the major university presidents immediately indicated it

was off the table. The goal of this is much more subtle.
It is to miseducate a generation of American/ college
students –

A/DAHNA. *(overlap)* Will you please let me ask my question!

B/VOICE OF ALAN DERSHOWITZ. *(overlap)* – so that when
they became the leaders ten, fifteen years down the
line, they would have a kind of knee-jerk opposition to
Israel of the kind that one sees in Europe –

A/DAHNA. *(overlap)* Will you please let me –

(Boos and jeers get louder.)

F/VOICE OF MODERATOR. I'm sorry, we'll have to move on
to the next question. I'm sorry.

A/DAHNA. I'm sorry too.

F/VOICE OF MODERATOR. There's a very long line of. People
are waiting, I'm sorry.

B/VOICE OF ALAN DERSHOWITZ. Sure.

F/VOICE OF MODERATOR. Yes, sorry. Our next question,
please?

(A exits to the last few waning catcalls.)

E/HORRIBLE MONSTER. This was not the end of our story,
dear Monsieur, but only the beginning. Listen as it
bleeds into another tale:

16. The Tale of Alan and Dahna, Part One

*(Outside the Dershowitz lecture at Columbia. **A/DAHNA**,
marches along, annoyed. It's early spring, chilly.)*

E/HORRIBLE MONSTER. Dahna was fair of countenance,
and her bravery made her enchanting to some. As she
left the great hall she caught the eye of the young Jew
called Alan.

*(**C**, as **ALAN**, runs up behind her.)*

C/ALAN. Uh, hi! Excuse me! Hi!

(She regards him evenly.)

C/ALAN. Hi. Uh, hi.

A/DAHNA. Hi.

C/ALAN. Hi. So that was uh great in there.

In that uh in the lecture you uh/ really held your own –

A/DAHNA. I didn't say anything.

C/ALAN. No, but you, you know, you stood your ground, and that's, that's.

I'm Alan.

(beat)

A/DAHNA. Dahna.

C/ALAN. Donna – like Donna?

A/DAHNA. DAH-na. D-A-H-N-A.

C/ALAN. Ah.

(pause)

C/ALAN. Anyway. I just wanted to let you know that we weren't all like. You know.

A/DAHNA. We?

C/ALAN. Jews.

I'm Jewish.

Also, my name is Alan.

A/DAHNA. Ah.

C/ALAN. I mean, he's kind of a jerk, you know. Dershowitz. We're not all.

A/DAHNA. I know you're not all.

(pause)

C/ALAN. I'm not making you aware of your otherness, am I?

A/DAHNA. Excuse me?

C/ALAN. Uh, I.

A/DAHNA. What is that supposed to mean?

*(**F** enters as a **STUDENT**, yelling.)*

F/STUDENT. Hey! You are a supporter of murderers and cancer. Do you know that?

C/ALAN. Will you excuse us, please?

F/STUDENT. You know what Israel's number one export is?

C/ALAN. Look, who cares what/ the export –

F/STUDENT. Medical technology! You are conspiring to keep medical tools out of the hands of sick people!

C/ALAN. *(suddenly very aggressive)* Fuck off!

F/STUDENT. *(trying to save face)* Just think about that.

(muttering to himself)

Typical Arab liar.

C/ALAN. Asshole!

(beat)

I'm sorry about that.

A/DAHNA. I'm used to it.

It sounded like you were going to get violent.

C/ALAN. Who, me? No.

A/DAHNA. You should be careful.

C/ALAN. What? No. Jews, we're loud, but we don't, we're not violent. We don't engage in violence.

A/DAHNA. Oh no?

(awkward silence)

C/ALAN. There's a place. In the West Twenties. Nobody knows about it but it's got the best sunsets in the world. You go up or down three blocks and it's not the same but that one spot. And at dusk, the sky turns a blue like you've never seen before.

A/DAHNA. Sure. Let's go.

Sure.

E/HORRIBLE MONSTER. And so the two sat, on the great Pier at Chelsea, and watched the sun set. Indeed it was superb as few sunsets are, worthy of the great desert to the East.

(A and C, as DAHNA and ALAN, on a park bench, as the sun sets. It's getting a little chilly. A/DAHNA smokes.)

A/DAHNA. You know, it's Kuwait, so. It's got to be something oil-related. Some trading thing, I bet. He doesn't talk much about his business with my sisters or me. I mean, he's supportive of us being in school and all, but you know, he's pretty traditional.

C/**ALAN**. Are there a lot of you?

A/**DAHNA**. Four girls.

A brother, but he died.

C/**ALAN**. I'm sorry.

A/**DAHNA**. It was before I was born.

C/**ALAN**. Are your sisters here too?

A/**DAHNA**. One of them's in Michigan, my older sister, she's married to this guy who owns a chain of gas stations. Another one's studying in Germany, the youngest one is in Kuwait with my parents.

We're lucky. We had some money. Family in all over the place, I came to Brooklyn when I was 11.

You're right, this is beautiful. Look at that sky. It's like a. Like a painting, like a deep blue canvas. If you shut your ears and pretended New Jersey wasn't there this could be the Nile, or the Jordan.

C/**ALAN**. I wish I could pretend New Jersey wasn't there.

A/**DAHNA**. New Jersey's okay.

C/**ALAN**. No, I'm from there. It's lame. You know.

(beat)

A/**DAHNA**. Listen, you want to go dancing?

C/**ALAN**. Dancing?

A/**DAHNA**. I got this e-mail, there's like this party collective thing happening out in Bushwick. Like someone turned an abandoned building into a club, with DJs and everything. But illegal. You down with that?

C/**ALAN**. Sure, I. Yeah, sure.

(**A/DAHNA** *laughs for no reason, long, loud, infectious.*)

A/**DAHNA**. Let's go, Jersey.

E/**HORRIBLE MONSTER**. And so they ventured through the regions of danger, through abandoned streets littered with trash and shattered glass, into the broken place of iniquity, to dance.

17. The Dance of Alan and Dahna

(**A** *and* **C** *dance, as* **DAHNA** *and* **ALAN**. *They should be alone on stage. The music should sound robotic and computerized, though catchy. Underneath the beeps and blips, perhaps we hear the light strains of Middle Eastern instruments, or perhaps the hypnotic voice of a Sufi singer. As the song progresses, the "artificial" music fades into the background and the Middle Eastern music becomes more dominant. It should sound like a collaboration between The Chemical Brothers and Nusrat Fateh Ali Khan.*)

(*It is important that Dahna, and especially Alan, not be trendy, or even particularly skillful dancers. They should, however, dance with complete, unselfconscious abandon. It's okay is they are a bit nervous at first, but that should gradually fall away. They should lose themselves in the dance, eyes half-closed, mouths half-open, laughing and sweating. It is goofy and sexy.*)

(*As the song becomes more Middle Eastern, actors drape the deep blue silk around them. They begin to spin, like Sufi dancers or whirling dervishes, spinning, spinning, spinning. The blue silk rises into the air.*)

(*They kiss.*)

(*As the music fades, they fall to the ground, asleep. Ensemble members cover them in deep blue silk.*)

(*The club is transformed into* **SHAHRIYAR**'*s palace.* **D** *enters, as* **DUNYAZADE**. *She stands over* **C**, *who is now* **SHAHRIYAR**, *and sleeping.* **A** *is now* **SCHEHERAZADE**.)

18. The Conspiracy of Scheherazade and Dunyazade

(*Some time has passed;* **DUNYAZADE** *is not as young as she was in the earlier scenes.*)

D/DUNYAZADE. Look at him. So vulnerable.

(**D** *picks up Shahriyar's scimitar.*)

A/SCHEHERAZADE. What are you doing?

D/DUNYAZADE. Oh. It's heavy.

(beat)

One swift stroke and it's him with no head.

A/SCHEHERAZADE. And then you would be stoned to death for treason.

D/DUNYAZADE. You would do that to me?

A/SCHEHERAZADE. What I would do is irrelevant. The law is the law.

D/DUNYAZADE. What law says he gets to murder every woman in the kingdom?

He wouldn't be missed. They hate him.

A/SCHEHERAZADE. They have almost forgotten about him.

D/DUNYAZADE. It has been a long time, hasn't it?

This is what you want? A prisoner of your own plan, trapped in a golden cage, telling one story after another to a man who will kill you once you run out of ideas? Because you will run out of ideas.

A/SCHEHERAZADE. Don't be so sure about that. Besides, you're in here with us almost every night.

D/DUNYAZADE. I like the stories.

A/SCHEHERAZADE. Well, then, perhaps you have some idea of why I do this.

What are any of us but a collection of stories? You change the story of a nation and you change that nation.

You had better put that back before he wakes up.

C/SHAHRIYAR. Put what back?

D/DUNYAZADE. Majesty!

C/SHAHRIYAR. Why does she have that? Why do you have that?

D/DUNYAZADE. Sister.

A/SCHEHERAZADE. *(winging it)* We were enacting a story. The tale of Sindbad. The sailor.

C/SHAHRIYAR. Is that a good one?

A/SCHEHERAZADE. *(putting her on the spot)* Is it, my sister?

D/DUNYAZADE. *(angry/scared)* Yes, sister. One of my favorites. Please, tell it from the beginning.

A/SCHEHERAZADE. Oh, his majesty was sleeping. Surely he does not want to hear another story.

C/SHAHRIYAR. No, that's okay. If it's a good one, I mean.

A/SCHEHERAZADE. Very well. Dunyazade, please, bring me that jar of sweet water. It appears I shall need my voice.

19. Sindbad the Seaman and Borges the Blind

*(**D** pours her water from a bowl as she narrates. **A** folds a little paper boat and puts it in the bowl.)*

A/SCHEHERAZADE. Long have men spoken of Sindbad the Seaman, Baghdadi merchant of legend, seven times lost to the ocean and seven times returned home, having seen infinite wonders:

*(**B** enters as **SINDBAD**, a shipwrecked medieval Iraqi merchant.)*

B/SINDBAD. It all starts to run together after a while: the waterfalls that run upward, the fish who recite poetry in beautiful feminine voices, the trains that move faster than the wind in a typhoon.

Seven times lost and seven times found. You start to wonder; am I doing somethiing wrong? Or something incredibly right?

Some things I remember:

Grapefruit trees and queer, flying hens.

A noise like a bomb going off and before I could take a breath we were all deep in icy-cold black water, searing pain in my sinuses, my eardrums like to burst, blood vessels in my eyeballs lacerating from the pressure.

Floating, starving, sunburned, skin peeling from my lips.

A fish with the head of an owl.

The tremendous, monolithic, unavoidable fact of my complete and utter aloneness.

Then Kardakhan, I saw some amazing things there. A rhinoceros, a Volkswagen, an Ikea. They would have you put together all this elaborate wooden furniture with this tiny little allen wrench. Really something.

Anyway, I saw lots more things, killed a bunch of people with a human leg-bone once, I'm not exactly proud of that.

Now? I'm stranded again, washed up on a rocky beach. There's an old man, sitting on a beach chair, wearing a suit, his hands folded at the top of his cane. He's looking at me, is he looking at me? No, he's blind. But he knows I'm here.

(Up on E, *as* **JORGE LUIS BORGES,** *the Argentinian author, at the end of his life, blind and using a cane. He sits as* **B** *described him.)*

B/SINDBAD. The blind man offers me pastries and thick-sweet Turkish coffee.

Who are you, I ask him.

E/BORGES. My advanced age has taught me the resignation of being Borges.

B/SINDBAD. He tells me,

E/BORGES. Jorge Luis Borges. Author and scholar. Born 1899, in Buenos Aires, died 1986, in Geneva. Liver cancer. I am not sure that I exist, actually. I am the writers that I have read, the women that I have loved; the cities that I have visited…

B/SINDBAD. He's a poet of some kind.

E/BORGES. There is a word, in my language: *mil-y-un-a-nocheso.* "One-thousand-and-one-nights-esque." Sometimes it is not the translation that is unfaithful to the original but the original that is unfaithful to the translation. Do you understand?

B/SINDBAD. I don't understand much. I just sort of go with it.

E/BORGES. You are not who you think you are. It was not Scheherazade who established the canon of the *Quitab alif laila ua laila,* The Book Of The Thousand Nights and One Night, but a Frenchman by the name of Jean

Antoine Galland, who added stories such as "Alaeddin and His Magic Lamp" and "Ali Baba and the Forty Thieves." His translation was then translated back into Arabic, where it replaced the original, if there ever was such a thing. But it was the English Captain Richard Burton who translated the tales into what they were all along: a repertory of marvels. Burton heaped onto Scheherazade's tales kisses, Viziers, palm trees, moons, with a stamina worthy of Cecil B. DeMille.

You, my dear Sindbad, are a story, someone's idea of a brackish picaroon adventurer, an example of a culture seen only from a distance. Though I suppose the same could be said about myself. Or about any of us.

(He indicates the audience. **SINDBAD** *thinks.)*

B/SINDBAD. You're freaking me out, Jorge Luis Borges.

E/BORGES. As usual I obscure more than I illuminate.

I wonder if we may posit a tale of a young couple in love, she an Arab, he a Jew, struggling to create themselves and each other even as history writes its own narrative deep into their skins. Let us call this tale

20. Alan and Dahna in Palestine

(A small home in Rafah, in Gaza, represented minimally. Sounds of gunfire outside. A comes running in as **DAHNA**, *holding a bundle representing a child. She ducks, as if she has been avoiding bullets.)*

A/DAHNA. Gaza.

It was his idea to come here.

(Sounds of gunfire continue from outside. Perhaps the bundle "cries.")

A/DAHNA. I had never even been here. We left the West Bank when I was four.

C/ALAN. *(V.O.)* You're the reason I want to go,

A/DAHNA. ...Exactly what I was hoping he wouldn't say. I'm not there, I thought, I'm here.

This is a bad night. We're walking home after curfew with

Mostafa, our translator, who has just taken his little girl to the Doctors Without Borders doctor. Something bad must have gone down today because soldiers start firing on us, that or they're just bored maybe, or scared, but we hear, pok! Pok! Pok! Little chunks fly out of stone walls over our heads, small clouds of dust appear at our feet.

I'm holding Mostafa's daughter, whose name I don't even know. I make a beeline for his front door, which is in sight.

A breath. Mostafa runs in behind me.

(**B** *runs in, as* **MOSTAFA**, *a thirtysomething Palestinian refugee. Beat.*)

A/DAHNA. *(to us)* No Alan.

(to **B***)*

Where's Alan?

B/MOSTAFA. *(Arabic accent, not too pronounced)* I don't know.

(They open the door and look out. From here to the end, intermittent gunshots.)

B/MOSTAFA. He's just standing there.

A/DAHNA. Why isn't he running? RUN, ALAN, I yell.

B/MOSTAFA. Sh. They are shooting at him. Above his head. If he does not move they will get closer and closer on his body until whoosh, right in his face.

A/DAHNA. RUN

B/MOSTAFA. Not so loud they will come here and suspect something.

I will get him.

A/DAHNA. You can't, I say.

B/MOSTAFA. Then your friend will die.

A/DAHNA. Let me go.

B/MOSTAFA. You?

I am not so traditional as some but I will not let a girl risk death because I am a coward. Especially a Arab girl.

Please. You do not want me to be a laughingstock among my friends.

A/DAHNA. Okay, I say. The seconds last forever, time slows down. Mostafa runs to the little white spot that's Alan and almost tackles him. Something happens. He's hit. He's doubled over, movement, they're arguing about something and they're coming, the bullets following them, they're here, I can see them, blood pouring from Mostafa's face, through Alan's Columbia sweatshirt.

*(**B/MOSTAFA** and **C/ALAN** enter. **B** has been shot in the eye. The actors may ad-lib freely here; this should be crosstalk.)*

B/MOSTAFA. *W'Allah yich-reb bet'hom el-yahud*

C/ALAN. I'm sorry I'm so sorry

A/DAHNA. What should we do

C/ALAN. It's his eye it's my fault just let's stop the bleeding

(sounds of the toddler crying)

A/DAHNA. It's okay honey sh

C/ALAN. Listen Mostafa can you hear me

B/MOSTAFA. I don't think it hit anything in the brain
In the cabinet in the back there's morphine

A/DAHNA. I run and get it. He has to talk us through how to administer it.
The blood looks worse than it is. He loses his eye, but four days later he'll be laughing about it. Anyway, his wife and all these other relatives wake up, they come in, take Mostafa I don't know where, elsewhere, and Alan and I are alone.

21. The Tale of Alan and Dahna, Part Two

*(**A** and **C**, as **ALAN** and **DAHNA**, cuddle under the blue silk.)*

C/ALAN. I couldn't move.

A/DAHNA. You were scared. It happens.

C/ALAN. It wasn't that. I wanted to draw his fire. I felt like he knew, the soldier, somehow, that you and Mostafa were Arabs and I was a Jew, that if I stood there he wouldn't kill me and you guys would. Get to safety.

But then it was a game of chicken, like I was calling his bluff. I had this whole fantasy where he kills me, it makes the news, a Jew kills another Jew, they argue about it in the Knesset.

Mostafa might die because of me.

A/DAHNA. He won't, I say, not knowing I would be right. Neither of us sleep that night.

22. The Tale of Alan and Dahna, Part Three

(Actors set the stage up, minimally, as **ALAN** *and* **DAH-NA'**s *apartment.)*

A/DAHNA. When we come back to New York, we move in together. I don't know if it's love that holds us together or something else. I tell myself it's love.

I am very afraid.

Alan avoids working on his thesis, I think it's about postcolonialism and internet porn. I avoid finishing an MFA nonfiction thesis. Which is on something else.

(C/ALAN *lounges on the couch, reading Borges'* Fic-ciones, *the blue silk balled up at his feet.)*

C/ALAN. Borges is fucking awesome. "The Library of Babel." Have you ever read that one?

A/DAHNA. Can't say I have.

C/ALAN. It's like this library the size of the universe where they have books containing every imaginable combination of letters, but because of that none of the books make sense. People spend their whole lives just trying to find a book that they can actually read.

A/DAHNA. *(not particularly interested)* Interesting.

Listen, I'm going to go out onto the fire escape and call my sister.

(no answer)

Alan?

C/ALAN. What?

A/**DAHNA.** I'll just be out here.

("climbs out;" to us)

This was the first time Asser was mentioned. Probably not the first but the first time I remember. I was on the phone with Lubna, my sister.

23. The Conspiracy of Dahna and Lubna, Part One

(She takes out a cell phone and dials. Up on **D** *as* **LUBNA,** *Dahna's sister. She is tacky and gaudy, like a New Jersey housewife; too much hairspray and jewelry. She has a faint Arabic accent.)*

D/**LUBNA.** It's what, now, eight years?

A/**DAHNA.** Six. Writing takes a long time.

(to us)

I'm not really writing anything.

D/**LUBNA.** Oh, you know who I just read? I forget her name, Sue, Susan, she writes the books where every book is a letter of the alphabet, A is for Alibi, B is for something…I just discovered her a few months ago and I'm already on N is For Noose.

A/**DAHNA.** Sue Grafton.

D/**LUBNA.** Yes, that's right. So smart. She's wonderful, you should write books like that.

A/**DAHNA.** How are the kids.

D/**LUBNA.** Oh, fine fine. Mohammed won the science award at his school and Fatima got on the soccer team, and little Ali is trying out for the school play, Pippin I think it's called, he's got such a lovely voice. He's not so little anymore either. Big Ali doesn't like it, he says it's decadent and he wants little Ali to play sports, maybe it's too feminine, I don't know. But listen, did you get Mommy and Dad's e-mail about Asser?

A/**DAHNA.** Who?

D/**LUBNA.** Dad's friend's son. The banker? Don't tell me you didn't get the e-mail.

A/DAHNA. I got *an* e-mail.

D/LUBNA. Did you open the attachment? He is so cute!

A/DAHNA. I'm not interested in an arranged marriage, Lubna.

D/LUBNA. Oh, so dramatic! No one is asking you to enter into an arranged marriage. He's rich, too.

A/DAHNA. Can we change the subject.

D/LUBNA. Dahna, I know your American boy is exciting, he went to Gaza with you (God knows why either of you would want to go to that awful place) but normal people's lives are not the movies! There's other reasons to settle down with a man besides that he's exotic.

(**DAHNA** *looks in at* **ALAN**, *reading and picking his nose.*)

A/DAHNA. He's not exotic.

D/LUBNA. Dad doesn't know you're living with him.

A/DAHNA. Are you asking me or telling me?

D/LUBNA. Mommy said she hasn't told him.

A/DAHNA. Let her tell him. Who cares?

D/LUBNA. He has too many worries already. Imagine if he knew you were living unmarried with a Jewish man?

A/DAHNA. That's his problem. Besides, Mahida's totally living with that Swedish guy.

D/LUBNA. That's different.

A/DAHNA. How is that different?

D/LUBNA. Listen, what is your instant message name?

A/DAHNA. My what?

D/LUBNA. Instant message! Like AOL or Yahoo. You can chat with Asser from London in "real time."

A/DAHNA. I don't have a. What am I, fifteen? I'm way too busy to spend my time instant messaging people.

(to us)

Another lie.

D/LUBNA. I'll make you one. It's fun. You'll see.

24. Open Sesame

(**DAHNA** *uses the Islamic tome as a laptop.*)

A/DAHNA. She makes me the screen name, like she said. It's shrzad1001, which I think is a reference to the Arabian Nights, and, because it's Lubna, it's of course embarrassingly cheesy.

(*pause*)

I admit that I sit and watch it and wait for words to appear in the little box.

(**F** *appears as* **ASSER,** *a handsome and wealthy English-Palestinian. He also has a laptop.*)

F/ASSER. (*English accent*)
>open sesame

A/DAHNA. Says the box. His screen name is alibabba423. I answer back with a question mark.

F/ASSER.
>a stupid joke, sorry
>the names
>i thought it was an interesting coincidence

A/DAHNA. Another question mark.

F/ASSER.
>the arabian nights?

A/DAHNA.
>don't know it
I type.
>i do like 19th-century british authors though
>austen dickens trollope
Which is mostly true. Nothing for a minute, then a quote from Jane Austen:

F/ASSER.
>"One does not love a place the less for having suffered in it, unless it has been all suffering, nothing but suffering."

A/DAHNA.

>you got that off your bookshelf

>i dont believe you memorized that

F/ASSER.

>guilty as charged

A/DAHNA.

>its on your bookshelf at least

>that counts for something

F/ASSER.

>actually i got it off google

A/DAHNA.

>philistine

F/ASSER.

>at least I'm honest and i'm cultured for a currency trader!!! i like opera. i just read a book about how terrible the international monetary fund is

A/DAHNA.

>what do you think about the imf?

F/ASSER.

>its awful but I make craploads of money because of it

>i'm not making a very good impression here am i

A/DAHNA.

>how much did lubna tell you about me

F/ASSER.

>you're an activist i find that very admirable

A/DAHNA.

>dont patronize me its boring

A pause, then:

F/ASSER.

>sigh

>look i'm totally uncomfortable with this

>it seems like the only choice i get is either being this rich arab playboy type serial dating blond europeans who have a palpable lust for my credit cards

>or i'm the traditionalist who enters into some arranged relationship with the daughter of his dads friend

>the truth is i'm lonely

>i love london but the weathers shite my jobs ok but i'd like to throw it all away and do development assistance for the third world

>but when i type that in it looks like i'm just trying to impress you

>and anyway i'll never do it because i like money too much

A/DAHNA. I don't type anything for a little while.

F/ASSER.

>hello

A/DAHNA.

>honesty is good

F/ASSER.

>dont patronise me its boring

A/DAHNA.

>i'm afraid you have begun to charm me, I type. Has he? Why did I type that?

F/ASSER.

>ah

A/DAHNA. The little box says, and right after that:

F/ASSER.

>do you want a picture of me

A/DAHNA.

>don't ruin it

F/ASSER.

>ha

A/DAHNA. But I'm surprised to find that I do want a picture of him. I do a search. there's a picture of me at a protest on some website. I find it, quickly scrolling by another picture of Alan and I holding a banner. I send him the link.

Nothing.

>too much?

I type.

I get a link back, click on it. It's to some corporation's
website. There he is, at some kind of a corporate party,
a handsome, well-groomed young Arab in a gray flan-
nel suit.

F/ASSER.

>too much?

A/DAHNA. I don't answer. He is gorgeous, which I'm surprised to find I care about.

F/ASSER.

>you're gorgeous

A/DAHNA.

>shut up

F/ASSER.

>seriously

A/DAHNA.

>i hadn't bathed a week in that pic

F/ASSER.

>imagine what you must look like when you're clean

A/DAHNA. I look back into my apartment.

What am I doing?

Alan stood there. In Rafah. He was ready to die for
me.

(Dahna's cell phone rings.)

25. The Conspiracy of Dahna and Lubna, Part Two

(It's LUBNA.)

D/LUBNA. Well?

A/DAHNA. Well what?

D/LUBNA. What do you think? Charming, right?

A/DAHNA. Who? Not you.

D/LUBNA. Very funny. Listen, Dahna, I don't know what
you think you're rebelling against.

A/DAHNA. I'm not rebelling against anything.

D/**LUBNA.** Just try to keep an open mind. Just because Asser's father is Dad's friend doesn't make him a bad guy.

A/**DAHNA.** Who said he was a bad guy?

D/**LUBNA.** Whatever. As long as you're happy.

A/**DAHNA.** *(to us)* Which means that she totally knows that I'm not happy. Which I'm not sure that I even know yet.

*(to **D**)*

I'm happy, I say.

26. The Tale of Dahna and Asser (Open Sesame, Part Two)

*(**DAHNA** at her laptop.)*

F/**ASSER.**

>hi again

A/**DAHNA.**

>asser i live with a guy

F/**ASSER.**

>your sister told me already

A/**DAHNA.**

>do you live with someone

F/**ASSER.**

>yes

A/**DAHNA.** In my chest there is an unexpected pang of jealousy.

F/**ASSER.**

>we're just friends you and i

>we're not even in the same country

A/**DAHNA.**

>is she english

F/**ASSER.**

>yes

A/DAHNA.

>is it serious

(to **E***)*

The cursor blinks at me for a while.

F/ASSER.

>is yours

A/DAHNA.

>i asked you first

F/ASSER.

>not really no

A/DAHNA. And then, right after:

F/ASSER.

>an ambivalent no

A/DAHNA.

>i'm ambivalent too

C/ALAN. Dahna?

A/DAHNA.

>gotta go more later

(She shuts the laptop/book. **ALAN** *sticks his head into the room.)*

C/ALAN. Have you seen that, what do you call it, uh, that uh thing?

A/DAHNA. Could you be more specific?

C/ALAN. The lamp thing.

A/DAHNA. What lamp thing?

C/ALAN. Never mind.

*(***ALAN** *exits. She opens the laptop.)*

A/DAHNA.

>you there?

F/ASSER.

>yes

A/DAHNA. I am becoming obsessed. I think constantly of what time it is in London versus what time it is here, whether he is at work or at home, if he's out, in a meeting, at lunch, asleep. With the English woman. Does he smell her blond hair? Will he tell her about me?

F/ASSER.

>yes

A/DAHNA.

>how do i know i can believe you

F/ASSER.

>i guess you just have to trust me

>i would like to see you

>i'm coming to new york next month

A/DAHNA.

>gotta go more later

(closes laptop)

27. The Tale of Alan and Dahna, Part Four Again, with Variations

(Noises/light of a TV. A/DAHNA, sits on a windowsill, smoking a cigarette out the window. C, still ALAN, uses the huge Islamic tome as if it is a laptop computer. A clicks a remote, turning off the TV.)

C/ALAN. I was watching that.

A/DAHNA. You're checking your e-mail.

C/ALAN. I was half-watching it.

A/DAHNA. What if I was gone?

C/ALAN. *(not paying attention)* Gone where.

A/DAHNA. What if that was all that was left of me? E-mail. Like if I went to Kuwait. Or back to Gaza, without you this time.

C/ALAN. Yeah.

I mean, I'm sorry, what?

A/DAHNA. Alan. There's something I have to tell you.

(C closes the book/laptop.)

C/**ALAN.** I'm sorry, that was rude of me. What were you saying?

A/**DAHNA.** I talked to my parents the other day.

C/**ALAN.** How are they?

A/**DAHNA.** They said they understood. What I was going through, my lifestyle, you know. They're not as. Intransigent. As you might think.

C/**ALAN.** I never thought they were intransigent.

A/**DAHNA.** They introduced me to this guy. An Arab guy, one of my Dad's friends.

C/**ALAN.** Okay.

A/**DAHNA.** We've been talking, online.

C/**ALAN.** Okay.

Is he in Kuwait?

A/**DAHNA.** London.

C/**ALAN.** So, what, is this like an arranged marriage kind of thing?

A/**DAHNA.** It's not that at all.

(The intercom buzzes.)

C/**ALAN.** Did you order something?

A/**DAHNA.** I got Casablanca. Remember? I asked you if you wanted something?

C/**ALAN.** Sorry.

(He buzzes the person in.)

C/**ALAN.** You were saying.

A/**DAHNA.** Nothing I.

I mean, what am I rebelling against?

C/**ALAN.** Um.

A/**DAHNA.** It's. Is this Western idea of dating really liberating? Or is it hegemonic?

C/**ALAN.** You want to talk about hegemony?

A/**DAHNA.** No, no. I mean, it would be one thing if I was living in Saudi Arabia or, but I'm not. I'm in New York. Where we're free to choose whatever we want as long as it's according to the dictates and the, uh, limits of the marketplace. But who's to say that's the best way?

C/**ALAN**. What are you. You're trying to tell me you want to leave me? Why don't you just break up with me instead of, of couching it in this cultural studies bullshit about hegemony, what the fuck is that?

A/**DAHNA**. Is that what you want, to break up?

C/**ALAN**. Of course not. I love you. I'm just, this is fucking weird.

A/**DAHNA**. Seriously, though, I mean. It's like. Everything we do, it's like it's not us doing it, like we're trapped in this grand narrative, or. And it's like, maybe we're trying to defy that narrative, or reinvent it, and I can't, I'm so exhausted, I just want to be normal.

C/**ALAN**. Everybody wants that.

A/**DAHNA**. Sometimes I wonder if I'm just some kind of Orientalist project for you.

C/**ALAN**. *(stunned)* I don't know know how to respond to that.

A/**DAHNA**. I'm sorry, that was. I didn't mean that how it sounded.

But I can't be who you want me to be.

It's like this thing is just a story that we're desperately trying to convince ourselves is true.

C/**ALAN**. I think it's true.

At least I thought it was.

Isn't everything a story?

(There's a knock at the door.)

C/**ALAN**. I got it.

(He moves to open the door.)

(BOOM!)

*(The windows implode. Broken glass and smoke shower the apartment. **ALAN** and **DAHNA** collapse. Something has exploded outside. It's major.)*

*(While they're on the floor, other cast members dress **A** and **C** as **SCHEHERAZADE** and **SHAHRIYAR**.)*

28. The Coming of the Crusaders (or, One Thousand Nights and One Night, Part Four)

(D comes running on, as **DUNYAZADE.***)*

D/DUNYAZADE. Scheherazade.

A/SCHEHERAZADE. Sister. What is happening?

D/DUNYAZADE. Great monstrous men have come on horseback. They spear infants on the end of their long thin swords. I have seen nothing like this.

(E enters, as **WAZIR.***)*

E/WAZIR. My lord. We must take flight.

C/SHAHRIYAR. What's going on?

E/WAZIR. Crusaders, majesty. These men know little of civilization, for theirs stopped evolving centuries ago and they remain as in ancient times.

(Commotion from outside. C goes to look.)

E/WAZIR. Don't! Lest you be skewered by a flaming arrow.

(Commotion gets closer.)

E/WAZIR. We must run.

C/SHAHRIYAR. No.

E/WAZIR. You do not wish to fight them. They are not human. They will cut us all and fornicate with our bleeding wounds.

C/SHAHRIYAR. I'm not going to fight.

E/WAZIR. They are not interested in your surrender.

C/SHAHRIYAR. The Queen was telling me a story. I need to hear how it ends.

E/WAZIR. A story? This is madness.

C/SHAHRIYAR. I'm not keeping you.

E/WAZIR. Scheherazade. Daughter. Come with us. He has no more power over you or anyone. His is a fallen kingdom.

C/SHAHRIYAR. You had best go now, Wazir. They are almost upon us.

A/SCHEHERAZADE. Go, father. I will stay with him.

E/WAZIR. I can not bear to think of what these animals will do to you.

D/DUNYAZADE. I want to stay too.

E/WAZIR. No!

C/SHAHRIYAR. Go or don't go, I don't care. Now, Scheherazade, time is short. I have to know how it all ends.

(**D** *and* **E** *leave, or not.*)

A/SCHEHERAZADE. Very well. A short tale for a short time. I bring you

29. The Tale of Alaeddin and His Magic Lamp

(**ALAN** *and* **DAHNA**'s *apartment again. The sound of the Crusaders turns into intermittent sounds of sirens below; it is midday, but there is no sun. Perhaps electricity in the building is out, or unreliable.* **C** *quickly becomes* **ALAN** *again, entering the apartment after a long abandonment, frantically looking for something. He wears a safety mask and perhaps goggles, or a gas mask.*)

A/SCHEHERAZADE. There once was a boy named Alaeddin, also known as Jew Alan, whose mind was addled by love, or a feeling that he had mistaken for love, so much so that he failed to notice the crumbling of the world around him.

C/ALAN. *(ad-lib as needed)* Okay…come on…okay.

A/SCHEHERAZADE. Deep within his lover's possessions was something that would allow him to understand why she wished to leave him, or something that would prevent her from leaving, or both.

(**C** *unearths the dusty, golden, bejeweled lamp.*)

C/ALAN. Okay.

(*He begins to furiously polish it with the blue silk.*)

A/SCHEHERAZADE. The object of his love was in possession of the Lamp of the Uncle, an object of great power that she was forbidden ever to use, for the price it exacted on its user was great.

C/ALAN. I don't care.

A/SCHEHERAZADE. Out from the Lamp of the Uncle came the Djinn of the Lamp, as Alaeddin hoped.

(**B** *enters, as* **DJINN.**)

B/DJINN. You have summoned me. I am your humble servant.

C/ALAN. I have a wish.

B/DJINN. That is why people summon me.

C/ALAN. I love someone. A woman, I want her back.

B/DJINN. You are sure that this is what you want?

C/ALAN. Yes.

(**B** *walks to the window and looks out on the chaos below.*)

B/DJINN. There has been great devastation visited upon your city. Many of your people are dead, or will be soon. Even within you, a sharp, vicious dust has entered your lungs and blood and stomach, a dust that will eat you from the inside and will one day prove your death.

I have but to inhale deeply and blow, and none of this will ever have happened. I can send a wind so strong that it gusts into the past, making one man miss his meeting with another man, or that goes even further back and kills a baby in his crib before he can grow into the man who drives the truck. But your small, soft heart will still be broken. Is this what you want? To keep your Dahna at your side, even in this fallen world?

(*beat*)

C/ALAN. We can move out of the city.

(*the* **DJINN** *disapproves*)

If this didn't happen it would have been something else anyway.

(*the* **DJINN** *disapproves; even more desperate*)

It's Bush's fault, the fucking idiot.

B/DJINN. (*to God*) *Bism'Allah, il rachman, il-raheem*, these men have never changed in the hundred thousand years since you have bid them walk. Why you have chosen them over us Djinn I shall never understand.

(beat)

It is done.

C/ALAN. Where is she?

B/DJINN. Patience. Your wish has been fulfilled. From when next you see your beloved to the end of your days, she shall remain by your side.

C/ALAN. Where can I find her?

B/DJINN. You would do well not to hasten this fate of yours.

She is on the emergency M106 bus arriving from the Bronx, hoping to salvage some of her belongings. If you leave now you will intercept her on the way here from Broadway.

30. The Tale of Alan and Dahna, Part Five

(C, as **ALAN,** *narrates his actions:)*

C/ALAN. There are emergency buses that shuttle people between the 110th street hot zone and points north. Like the genie said, an M106 pulls up to the corner. It's like a clown car, dozens of people piling off of this city bus, all in masks. The bus has its headlights on because it's pitch black at two in the afternoon.

No Dahna.

Was the genie lying to me? No, there she is, scrambling to get off, pushing her way through the throngs of refugees. The smell of fear and grief that wafts from them is so strong it almost drowns out the fumes.

The bus jerks to a stop about halfway up the block and Dahna shoves her way out. She marches up the hill, carrying an empty duffel bag.

Dahna.

*(***DAHNA*** enters, as* **ALAN** *described. She wears the deep blue cloth as a mask; it looks like a veil, perhaps that worn by Kuchuk Hanem earlier.)*

A/DAHNA. Hi.

C/**ALAN**. Where are you staying.

(beat)

A/**DAHNA**. Queens.

I just came back to get some stuff.

You really shouldn't be here, Alan. Manhattan is uninhabitable.

C/**ALAN**. You didn't come back for me?

A/**DAHNA**. I really can't think about this now, Alan.

C/**ALAN**. He lied.

A/**DAHNA**. Go to New Jersey. Your family must be worried sick. There are ferries. You can go to Riverbank Park, the Army's taking people over in helicopters.

C/**ALAN**. Can I stay with you?

(**F** *approaches them as the* **COLUMBIA STUDENT** *from earlier. He, too, wears a safety mask.*)

F/**STUDENT**. Ah, excuse me.

A/**DAHNA**. I don't think that would be a good idea.

I'm staying with cousins. They're very conservative. And frankly scared out of their fucking minds.

F/**STUDENT**. Excuse me?

C/**ALAN**. It wasn't a big deal in Gaza.

A/**DAHNA**. They're not fucking refugees, Alan. They own a bodega.

F/**STUDENT**. Excuse me, I.

C/**ALAN**. Can you see we're talking here?

(**F** *lifts* **A**'s *veil.*)

A/**DAHNA**. Hey –

C/**ALAN**. What the fuck –

F/**STUDENT**. I thought so. You fucking terrorist cunt.

C/**ALAN**. Hey, fuck off, we're trying to have a conversation.

F/**STUDENT**. They think a million people. Because of Arab scum like you.

C/**ALAN**. Fuck you.

(**F** *takes out a brick.*)

F/STUDENT. This is all that's left of my work.

C/ALAN. Calm down, man, don't be a dick.

F/STUDENT. Fucking brain you.

> (ALAN *shoves him, hard. Beat. The student hits him in the head with the brick. There's blood.*)

F/STUDENT. (*scared by what he just did*) Yeah okay

> (*He swings at* **DAHNA.** *Quickly, she takes Shahriyar's sword from her duffel bag and slices his arm off with it.*)

F/STUDENT. Uh

A/DAHNA. Run

> (*He takes off.* **DAHNA** *suddenly forgets how to use the sword and drops it, shocked that she had it. She kneels down to* **ALAN.**)

A/DAHNA. Alan.

Alan.

Alan.

Wake up.

Alan.

Alan.

B/DJINN. Your wish is my command.

> (*He takes the sword and the severed arm and disappears.*)

31. One Thousand Nights and One Night, Part Five

> (*A hospital room, elsewhere, some time later. It is no longer dark, though it isn't exactly light either.* **DAHNA,** *still wearing her veil [though it is perhaps partially off], sits at the side of the bed where* **ALAN** *lies, hooked up to all manner of gadgets. Perhaps it is unclear where/when we are; elements may remain from the Scheherazade story.*)

> (**DAHNA** *reads to* **ALAN** *from the enormous Islamic tome.*)

A/DAHNA. And so it was Scheherazade bore the King three boy children. She set them before the King, saying:

(as **SCHEHEREZADE***)*

"O king, these are thy children and I crave that thou release me from my doom; for an thou kill me they will become motherless."

(as **DAHNA***)*

When the King heard this, he wept, and straining the boys to his bosom, he said: "By Allah, O Scheherazade, I pardoned thee long before the coming of these children!"

Shahriyar summoned chroniclers and bade them write all that had betided his wife, first and last; so they wrote and named it *The Stories of the Thousand Nights and One Night.* The book came to thirty volumes and these the King laid up in his library.

(She shuts the book. Beat.)

A/DAHNA. The book came to encompass every word ever written and the King's treasury grew to the size of the world. The story became us. Scheherazade writes us still.

(beat)

The book was a trap, designed as a prison of words to tell us who we are and what we can or cannot do. There is no way to break free of this prison.

(beat)

The book was meant as a joke but it got mistaken for history.

(Beat. She kisses blue silk and tenderly lays it over him, like a blanket. Beat.)

*(***D** *enters, as* **LUBNA***. She wears parts of a chemical suit reminiscent of the burqa she wore as Dunyazade.)*

D/LUBNA. You almost ready?

A/DAHNA. Sure.

(to C)

See you tomorrow.

D/LUBNA. Tch.

You're so young. Pretty.

Every day you're in this hospital room with him.

You can't waste your youth in here. What if he never gets better?

A/DAHNA. Shut up, Lubna.

(They exit. Beat.)

(The music from the Dance of Alan and Dahna plays. C rises from his bed and dances, like a Sufi. A enters and dances with him.)

(They dance.)

End of play

SELECTED BIBLIOGRAPHY/SUGGESTIONS FOR FURTHER READING OR VIEWING

The Arabian Nights: Tales From The Thousand and One Nights, Modern Library Edition, translated by Sir Richard F. Burton

Orientalism, Edward Said

Reading Lolita in Tehran, Azar Nafisi

Flaubert in Egypt, Gustave Flaubert

Arabian Nights and Days, Naguib Mahfouz

If on a winter's night a traveler, Italo Calvino

Invisible Cities, Italo Calvino

The Woman Who Pretended to be Who She Was, Wendy Doniger

The Satyricon, Petronius

Persuasion, Jane Austen

"The Blood of the Walsungs," Thomas Mann, published in *Death in Venice and Other Stories*

"The Albertine Notes," Rick Moody, published in *The McSweeney's Mammoth Treasury of Thrilling Tales*

"The Translators of The Thousand and One Nights," Jorge Luis Borges, published in *Selected Non-Fictions*

A Midsummer Night's Dream, William Shakespeare

The Tintin Adventures, Herge

Persepolis, Marjane Satrapi

Palestine, Joe Sacco

Vertigo, directed by Alfred Hitchcock, screenplay by Alec Coppel & Samuel Taylor, from the novel *d'Entre les Morts*, by Pierre Boileau and Thomas Narcejac

Casablanca, directed by Michael Curtiz, screenplay by Howard Koch and Julius & Philip Epstein

Dark Days, directed by Marc Singer

The International Solidarity Movement website, http://www.palsolidarity .org

From the Reviews of **1001...**

"Jason Grote is one of a generation of brainy new American dramatists –
including Tracy Letts and Will Eno – who understand that to reach new
audiences, political theater needs to move beyond moral indignation
and outrage, past spoon-feeding an attitude. One key to going forward is
looking backward into literature, fable and allegory."

- LA Weekly

"...a wild and beautiful glimpse at the yarns that shape our lives...
Even if it isn't always true, the story we keep telling – about the
power of love, violence, and death – is a comfort. Grote tackles that
concept with gripping imagination, achieving a cosmic scope by
eliminating the barriers between worlds."

- Variety

"Grote's Orientalist fantasia...conjures a storybook world that
dissolves, at a moment's notice, into an apocalyptic, 21st-century
landscape. Where to begin to describe this seductive if smart-
alecky, nonlinear play? ...[*1001*] doesn't preach, and it doesn't
underestimate the audience's intelligence."

- Washington Post

"There once was, praise Allah, a Jason Grote. This Grote lived in the
utmost wilderness (a/k/a Brooklyn) where he read many authors
– Benjamin, Said, Borges, Gramsci – and watched many videos
– Vertigo, Monty Python and the Holy Grail, Thriller. One day, he
combined these various influences into a play, loosely based on Sir
Richard Burton's Arabian Nights. Grote called this play *1001*."

- Village Voice

"In Jason Grote's kaleidoscopic reinvention of the "1001 Nights"
tales, [Scheherezade] morphs into Dahna, a contemporary
Palestinian graduate student in New York, just as Scheherazade's
husband, the wife-killing Shahriyar, becomes Dahna's Jewish
boyfriend, Alan, and her sister Dunyazade becomes Dahna's sister,
Lubna. Moving fluently back and forth from the "Arabian Nights" of
legend (complete with jeweled turbans and scimitars) to New York
in a dusty, apocalyptic near-future, these stories within stories come
to include Flaubert during his wild-oats days in Egypt and even a
cameo appearance by Jorge Luis Borges, the master of labyrinthine
fictions."

- New York Times

"The first production to come out of Denver Center Theatre
Company's New Play Summit is a riot of ideas, experiences and
influences...*1001* brings forth a thrilling night in the theater, one in
which the senses and the mind race..."

- Rocky Moutain News

From the Reviews of **1001...**

"...always fascinating...*1001* is an ambitious and risk-taking play
that makes quite a few demands on the audience."
- *Los Angeles Times*

"Through the filter of the ideas of Edward Saïd, and the
wordplay of Jorge Luis Borges (whose ghost makes a cameo),
the cast of six takes on the roles of 27 characters that beg the
question, 'What are any of us, but a collection of stories?'
Through these interchanging roles, the equally elaborate and
understated costumes, and subtle video projections, the tales
readily consume the audience."
- Flavorpill

"Grote explores some sophisticated questions — most notably
how do Americans rewrite and retell our own Arabic narratives
in the post-Sept. 11 world? Furthermore, how can we trust a
history — with no "true" referent — that changes with every
retelling? (Thankfully, no answers are ever provided.)"
- *Back Stage*

"*1001* was the most exciting offering of the recent Denver Center
Theatre Company season."
- *The Denver Post*

OTHER TITLES AVAILABLE FROM SAMUEL FRENCH

EVIL DEAD: THE MUSICAL
Book & Lyrics By George Reinblatt
Music By Frank Cipolla/Christopher Bond/Melissa Morris/
George Reinblatt

Musical Comedy / 6m, 4f / Unit set
Based on Sam Raimi's 80s cult classic films, *Evil Dead* tells the
tale of 5 college kids who travel to a cabin in the woods and
accidentally unleash an evil force. And although it may sound
like a horror, its not! The songs are hilariously campy and
the show is bursting with more farce than a Monty Python
skit. *Evil Dead: The Musical* unearths the old familiar story:
boy and friends take a weekend getaway at abandoned cabin,
boy expects to get lucky, boy unleashes ancient evil spirit,
friends turn into Candarian Demons, boy fights until dawn
to survive. As musical mayhem descends upon this sleepover
in the woods, "camp" takes on a whole new meaning with up-
roarious numbers like "All the Men in my Life Keep Getting
Killed by Candarian Demons," "Look Who's Evil Now" and
"Do the Necronomicon."

Outer Critics Circle nomination for
Outstanding New Off-Broadway Musical

"The next Rocky Horror Show!"
- New York Times

"A ridiculous amount of fun."
- Variety

"Wickedly campy good time."
- Associated Press

Breinigsville, PA USA
27 January 2010
231442BV00004B/20/P